The Queen Of Hearts

by Caldecott

THE QUEEN OF HEARTS.

THE Queen of Hearts,
She made some Tarts,

All on a Summer's Day:

The Knave of Hearts,
He stole those Tarts,

11

And took them right away.

The King of Hearts,
Called for those Tarts,

And beat the Knave full sore:

The Knave of Hearts,
Brought back those Tarts,

And vowed he'd steal no more.